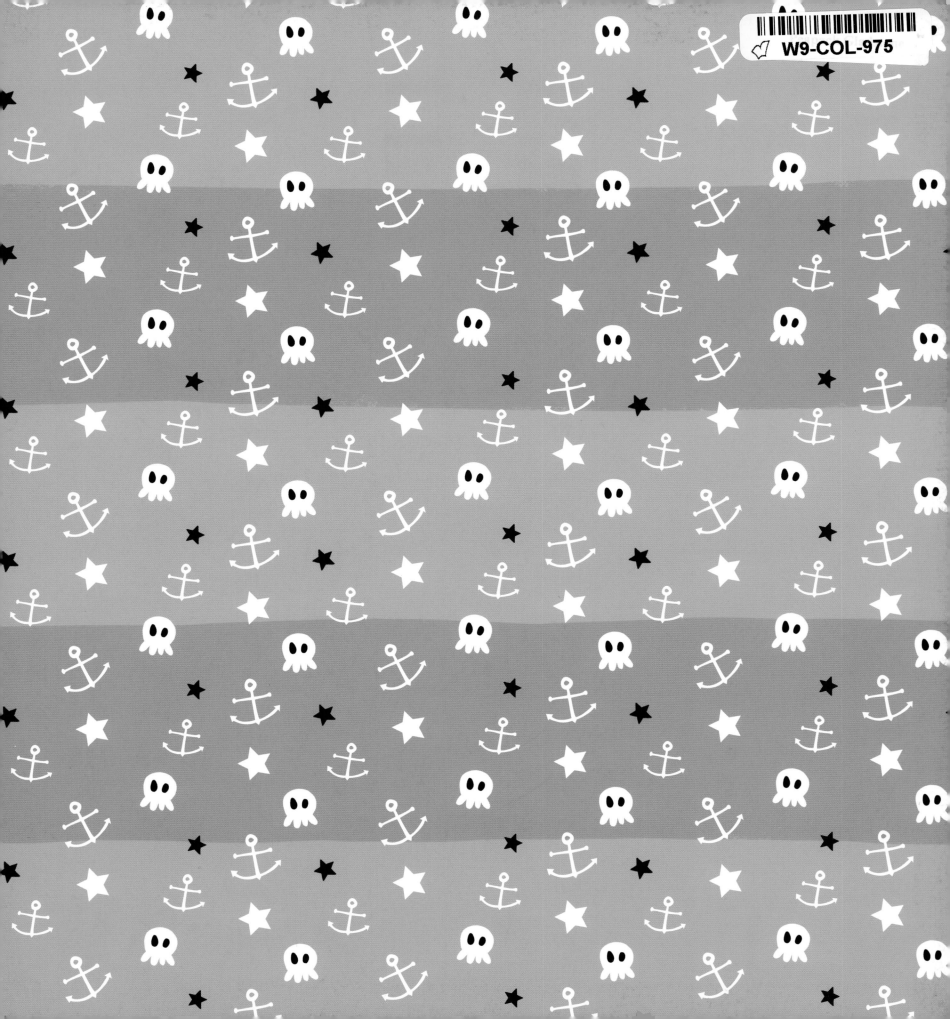

This book be for
Luca, Emilio, Lewis, Shaun, Lily, Mum, Dad
and all me shipmates!

And for you!

tiger tales
5 River Road, Suite 128, Wilton, CT 06897
Published in the United States 2013
Originally published in Great Britain 2013
by Caterpillar Books
Text and illustrations copyright © 2013 Maxine Lee
CIP data is available
CPB/1800/0255/0313
ISBN-13: 978-1-58925-143-4
ISBN-10: 1-58925-143-1
Printed in China
CPB/1800/0255/0313
For more insight and activities,
visit us at www.tigertalesbooks.com

Pi-Rat!

by Maxine Lee

HERE BE PIRATES!

tiger tales

A pirate's life for us!

No. 1 pirate!

There be no rules on my mighty ship!

Whatever We

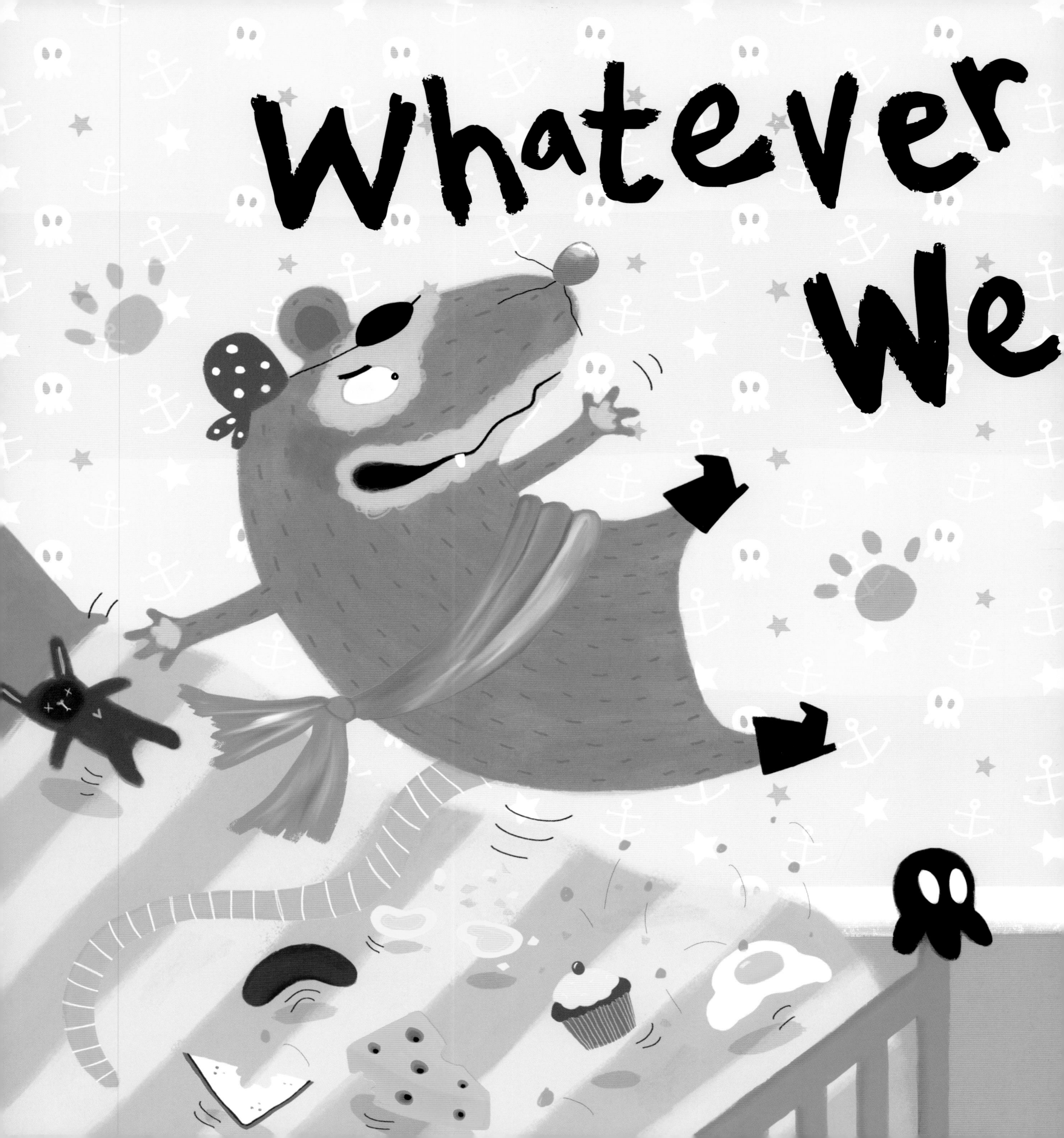

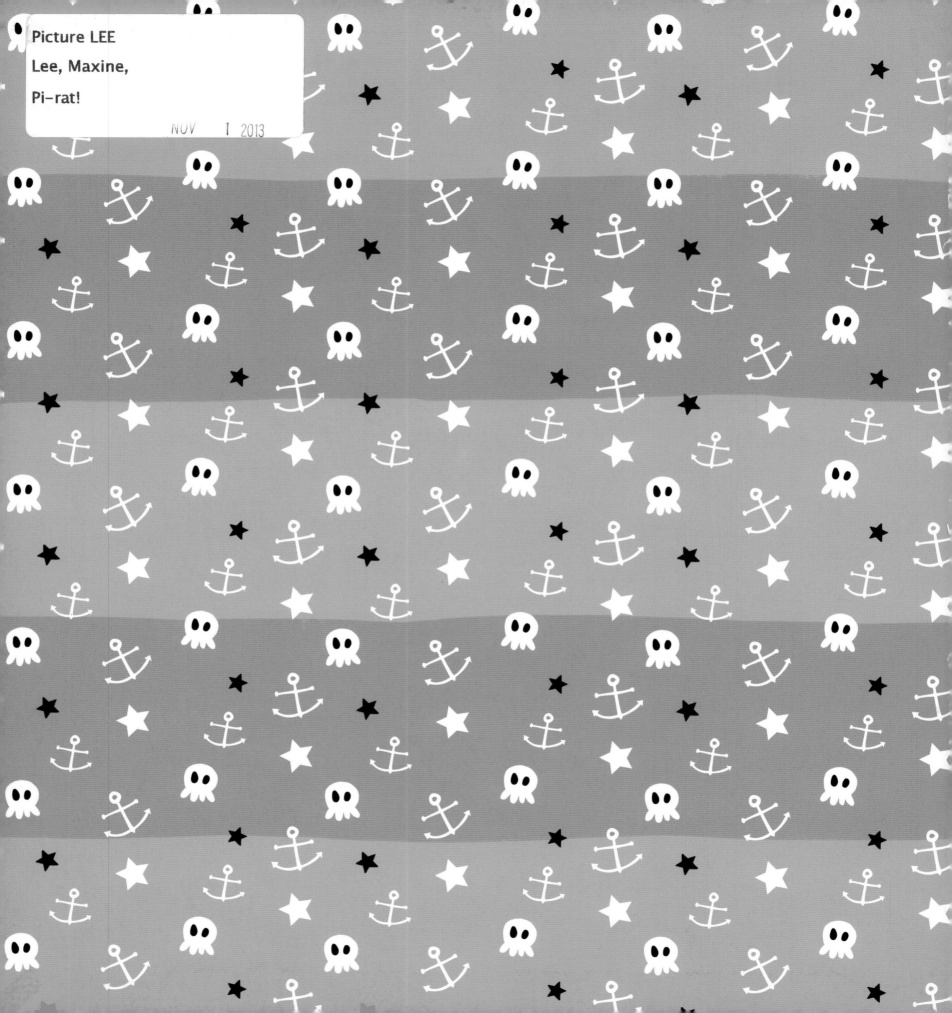